Where in the world is Henry?

BRADBURY PRESS · SCARSDALE, NEW YORK

The text of this book is hand-lettered.
The illustrations are pencil drawings with one-color line overlays,
reproduced in line and halftone.

For Hank

Where in the World is Henry?

I think he's
under the quilt.

Where is the quilt?

The quilt
is
on the
bed.

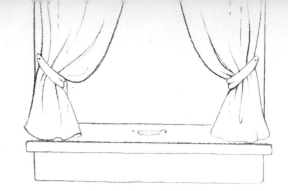

Where is the bed?

The bed is in the bedroom.

Where is the bedroom?

The
bedroom
is in
the
house

Where is the house?

The house is on the street.

Where *is* the street?

The
street
is in
the
town.

Where is the town?

The town is in the state.

Where is the state?

The
state
is in
the
country.

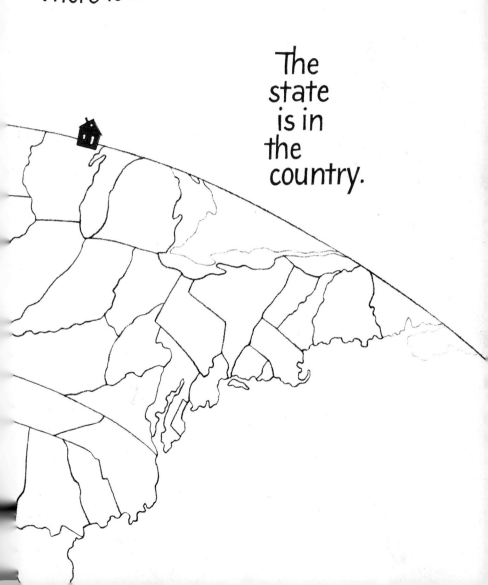

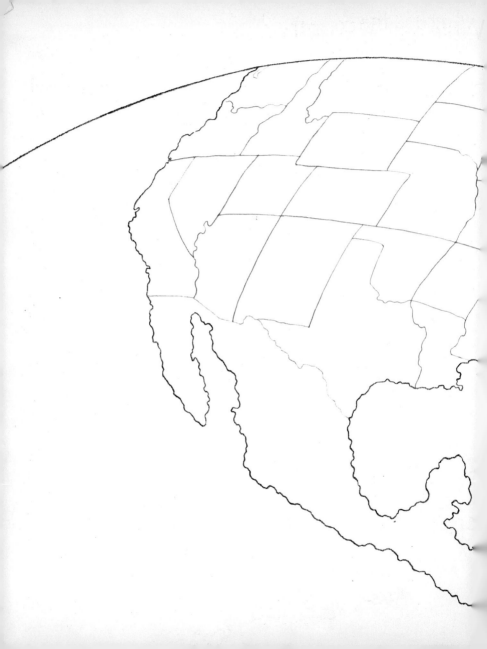

Where is the country?

The country is on the continent.

Where is the continent?

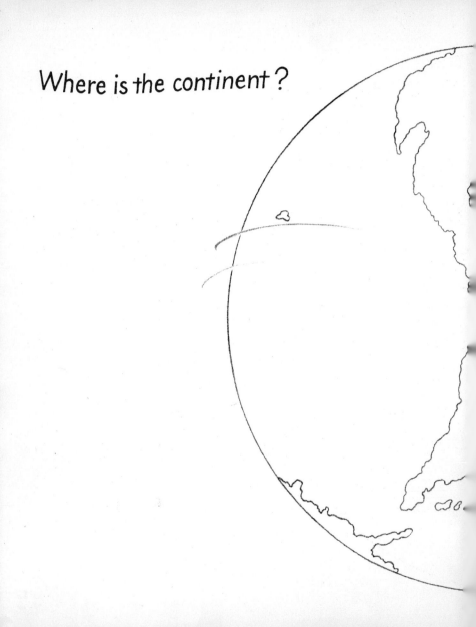

The
continent
is on
the planet.

Where is the planet?

It's spinning around in the universe.

What is the universe?

The universe is all of everything —
everywhere.

But where is Henry?

Come out of there,

Henry!

c.1

E
B

Balian, Lorna
  Where in the world is Henry?   Bradbury,
1972.
unp. illus.

  The question in the title leads a
sister to answer a younger brother about
Henry's relative whereabouts under a
quilt, in a room, in a house, in a town,
in a country, on a continent, on a planet,
in the universe.